SKY

All About Planets, Stars, Galaxies, Eclipses and More

David Allen

Illustrated by Ron Galimam

Greey de Pencier Books

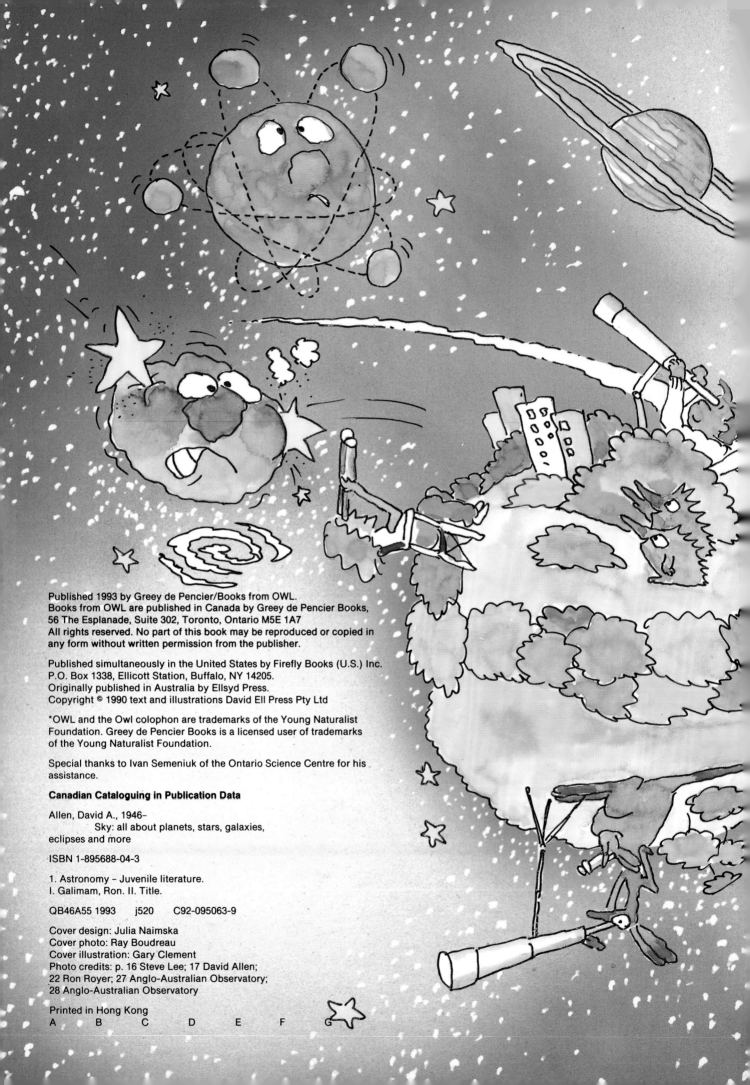

Published 1993 by Greey de Pencier/Books from OWL.
Books from OWL are published in Canada by Greey de Pencier Books,
56 The Esplanade, Suite 302, Toronto, Ontario M5E 1A7

Published simultaneously in the United States by Firefly Books (U.S.) Inc.
P.O. Box 1338, Ellicott Station, Buffalo, NY 14205.
Originally published in Australia by Ellsyd Press.
Copyright © 1990 text and illustrations David Ell Press Pty Ltd

*OWL and the Owl colophon are trademarks of the Young Naturalist
Foundation. Greey de Pencier Books is a licensed user of trademarks
of the Young Naturalist Foundation.

Special thanks to Ivan Semeniuk of the Ontario Science Centre for his
assistance.

Canadian Cataloguing in Publication Data

Allen, David A., 1946–
        Sky: all about planets, stars, galaxies,
eclipses and more

ISBN 1-895688-04-3

1. Astronomy – Juvenile literature.
I. Galimam, Ron. II. Title.

QB46A55 1993   j520   C92-095063-9

Cover design: Julia Naimska
Cover photo: Ray Boudreau
Cover illustration: Gary Clement
Photo credits: p. 16 Steve Lee; 17 David Allen;
22 Ron Royer; 27 Anglo-Australian Observatory;
28 Anglo-Australian Observatory

Printed in Hong Kong
A   B   C   D   E   F   G

Contents

Observatories

Have you ever seen an observatory?

Like fairy-tale castles, they are usually built on high mountains. This is because the air we breathe shimmers a lot and makes faint stars hard to see.

Observatories are also built a long way from cities because lights make the sky too bright to see faint stars.

Inside each observatory dome is a telescope used by astronomers to find out about stars, galaxies and planets. This book describes some of the things that astronomers have learned.

Inside the control room

Professional astronomers don't look through telescopes. Instead they work all night in a comfortable control room.

A computer directs the telescope to point at the right star and gathers the information that the telescope and its instrument collect.

A night assistant controls the telescope all night. He or she makes sure that it is working properly and that it is pointing at the star or galaxy that the astronomer wants to observe.

The astronomer operates another computer. This controls the instrument that analyzes the light collected by the telescope.

1. Light comes in here.

3. A second mirror focuses the light down through a hole in the middle of the main mirror.

4. The light comes into an instrument that measures it and sends the information to a computer.

2. A glass mirror under here can be as big as 10 m (30 feet) across. It sends light back up the telescope.

Telescopes

There are two types of telescopes. The big one in the observatory dome is a **reflecting telescope**. The light is reflected off mirrors. Some amateur astronomers have small telescopes of this type.

Refracting telescopes are the other type. They have a glass lens at the big end, and you look through a small lens — called the eyepiece — at the other end. A few professional telescopes are of the refracting type.

Some big telescopes have a smaller one attached to help you point at things in the sky. This is called a **finder**.

Most astronomical telescopes turn things upside down! Other telescopes use a different eyepiece so that the view is the right way up.

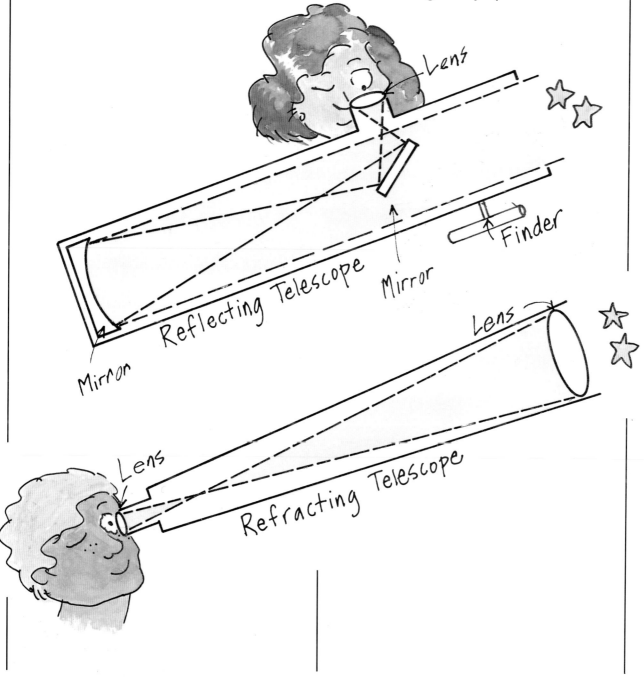

Lens

Finder

Reflecting Telescope

Mirror

Mirror

Lens

Lens

Refracting Telescope

The Solar System

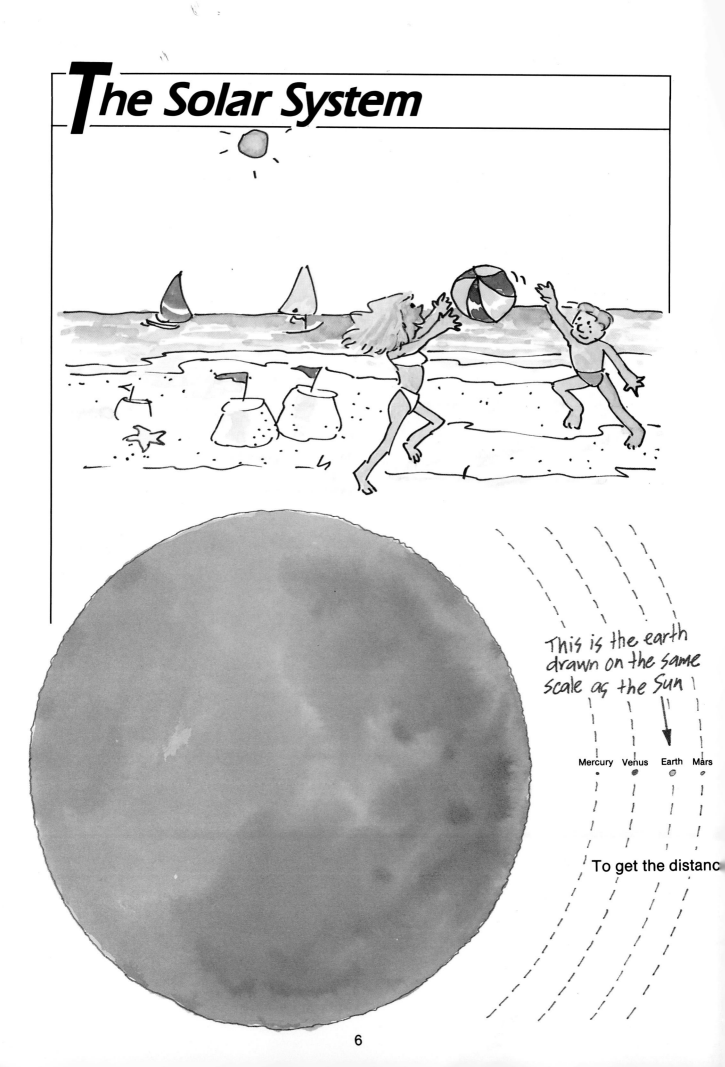

This is the earth drawn on the same scale as the Sun

Mercury   Venus   Earth   Mars

To get the distanc

To us, the earth is the most important place. The sun and moon are small objects lost in a big, blue sky. The earth seems very big indeed, and it is hard to imagine that the sun could be any bigger.

In fact, the sun is a big, hot star. The earth and moon are a couple of tiny lumps of rock in a family of planets that accompany the sun on its journey through space.

Astronomers call the sun and its planets the **solar system**. They think of it as such a tiny patch of the universe that it is like a backyard to the earth. But the distances are huge: from the earth to the sun is 150 million km (93 million miles). If you could fly to the sun in a jet aircraft, even without stopping it would take over 20 years.

The earth goes around the sun once a year. This is called **orbiting**. We know of nine planets that orbit the sun.

In order outwards they are:
Mercury
Venus
Earth
Mars
Jupiter
Saturn
Uranus
Neptune
Pluto

Most of the planets have smaller moons orbiting them. Earth has only one moon but Jupiter and Saturn have nearly 20 moons each.

A **star** is a very large body in space that glows and gives off light.

A **planet** is a large body that orbits around a star, but does not give off light of its own.

A **moon** is a smaller body that orbits around a planet.

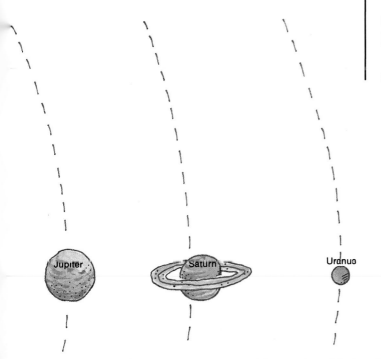

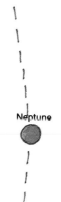

etween the sun and earth right on this scale, think of the earth being 15 m (50 feet) away.

The Sun

The surface of the sun is so hot that every known material would not just melt there, but boil. Inside the sun is much, much hotter still.

At its center the sun is like a giant hydrogen bomb continually exploding. Every single second of every day, several thousand million tons of hydrogen gas are turned into helium gas. It is this process that gives off the enormous heat which keeps our planet warm, even though we are so far away.

Prominences

Although the sun is round, like a ball, special telescopes show that from time to time giant clouds and streaks of hot gas burst out from the sun's surface like flames. These are called **prominences**.

Sunspots

Sunspots are cooler patches on the sun that appear dark. Actually they are hot and bright, but not as hot and bright as their surroundings. Sunspots also act like giant magnets. If you could take a compass to the sun you would find the needle pointing almost straight down into sunspots.

The number of spots on the sun changes. Some years there are lots, some years there are few. Times of plenty come about every 11 years: sunspots were very common in 1980 and 1991 and will be again around 2002. In between these years they will be much rarer.

Sunspots affect the earth. When there are lots of spots on the sun we often have difficulty receiving radio signals from far away.

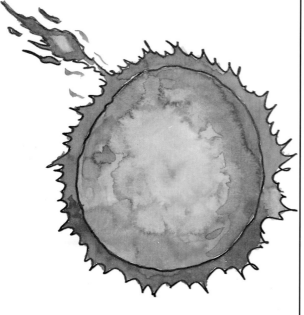

Watching the Sun

Never look at the sun for more than a second or two. The sun's heat can burn the inside of your eyes very quickly. Even sunglasses aren't dark enough to make it safe to stare at the sun.

Telescopes and binoculars concentrate the heat from the sun more, so **never look at the sun through any type of telescope**. Here is a safe way to look at the sun. Ask an adult to help you the first time.

1. Point your telescope roughly towards the sun. If you are using binoculars, cover one front lens.

2. Hold a piece of white card close to the eyepiece.

3. Tilt your telescope around till its shadow on the card is perfectly round. This means that it is pointing straight at the sun. When you have lined up, you will see a bright spot in the middle of the shadow. Now leave your telescope still.

4. Move the white card back 1 to 2 m (4 to 5 feet). The bright spot grows into a round patch of light as you do. Adjust the focus of the telescope until the round patch has sharp edges. This is an image of the sun. You may then see sunspots on the image. Stand the card up and shade it with a blanket to see the sun's image better.

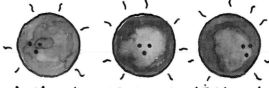

10 March   13 March   15 March

Try keeping a log of your observations of the sun. Make a drawing of where the spots are every clear day for a week or two. Try to observe the sun at about the same time every day. You will see the spots move across the sun as it rotates. The sun takes about one month to go around once.

Day and Night

Why the sky is blue

Light is what lets us see things and their colors. When the sun is shining we see green leaves, brown earth, blue sky and many other things. We don't think of light itself as having any color at all, but it does. Sunlight is actually a mixture of colors jumbled together: red, orange, yellow, green, blue, indigo and violet.

Sometimes when light passes through raindrops, it bounces off the water and breaks up into all the different colors that are in it. We see them as a rainbow.

Something like this happens when light passes through air. The air we breathe is made up of lots of tiny particles of gas. When light tries to go past them, they act like little mirrors and reflect part of the light, the blue part, to one side. In fact, the particles do such a good job of bouncing the blue light back and forth in the air that it seems to come from all over the sky.

Sunset

When the sun gets very low in the sky, its light passes through much more air. Yellow, orange, and even red light begin to reflect off the particles in the air, and so the sun and sky may appear red at sunset.

As darkness falls, the twilight glow settles in the west. You can also see another faint glow called the zodiacal light. This is caused by zillions of tiny bits of dust (left behind by comets) around the sun, far away from planet earth. Early spring is the best time to see the zodiacal light.

The shadow of the earth

About 15 minutes after sunset, look for the shadow of the earth in the eastern sky. The shadow is cast on the air itself and on the smoke and dust it contains. The dark part is the shadow of the earth; the pink part above is dust that can still see the sun low in the west, so its red light gets through.

11

Time

If you ride on a merry-go-round, everything seems to be going around you. Of course, you are the one going around.

The earth is our merry-go-round. As it turns, the rest of the universe seems to circle around it. During the day, the sun moves steadily across the sky. We set our clocks by the sun, counting 24 hours each time the earth spins.

Making a sundial

A sundial uses the sun's position to tell the time. To make a sundial, choose a sunny spot and push a post into the ground so that it points towards the North Pole of the sky. Page 26 tells you how to find that.

If you mark where the shadow of the post is at 10 a.m. one day, it will get back to the marker at 10 a.m. the next day. You can use sticks or stones to mark the hours.

Your sundial won't keep perfect time. It will read a little late in January and February and a little early in October and November, because the earth neither orbits the sun in a perfect circle nor at a steady speed.

If each marker represents an hour, what time does this sundial show?

To North Pole of sky

Gnomon

Support

Afternoon side

North

Midday Line

Morning side

Marker

Star time

Star time is a different time from sun time. Choose a bright star that you can see out of a south-facing window. Move your head till the star just disappears behind the window frame. Make a pencil mark on a piece of tape stuck to an item of furniture so that it lines up with the star and the window frame. Note the exact time.

Try again the next clear night. You will find that the star gets to the same place four minutes earlier every day. (If it doesn't, you may be tracking a planet instead of a star.)

The star clock keeps a different time because the earth orbits the sun. Stars must cross the sky faster than the sun so that they can make an extra circuit of the sky each year. The stars that you see at sunset one month will set two hours before the sun does a month later, so you see different groups of stars at different times of the year.

I'm a winter star. I can't stand hot summer nights.

I'm a summer star. You won't see me on a winter night.

The Moon

The moon takes one month to orbit the earth. The word "month" means "of the moon".

The moon is much bigger and further away than it looks. It's one-quarter as big across as the earth. If someone could build an expressway to the moon, it would take five months of non-stop driving to get there. You'd also need nearly three days to drive around the moon. When you finally arrived you'd find it pretty boring — nothing but dry soil, gentle hills and a few boulders; no water, no grass, no houses, no animals. Even the famous craters are only shallow hollows with low hills around them.

The man in the moon

The dark patterns that form the face of the man in the moon are huge plains that were formed when molten rock poured out of cracks in the surface. The cracks were made when big lumps of rock crashed into the moon and made the craters. All this happened over 4000 million years ago.

MOON
No fuel or water
for next 400,000km
(250,000 miles).

Full moon

The moon is round, like a ball, so only one half is lit up by the sun and the other half is dark. When there is a full moon, we see the whole section that is sunlit.

During the two weeks of each "day" on the moon, the temperature rises to boiling point — you could fry eggs on the rocks — and during the two weeks of "night" it gets colder than any place on earth, even the South Pole.

New moon

When the moon is new, we look at its dark side. If you were standing up there you would see a fully lit earth in the sky, four times as big and much brighter than the full moon looks to us. In fact the earth gives the moon some light at night. Watch for the dark side glowing dimly when the moon is a narrow crescent, just after new moon. This is called earthshine, or "the old moon in the new moon's arms".

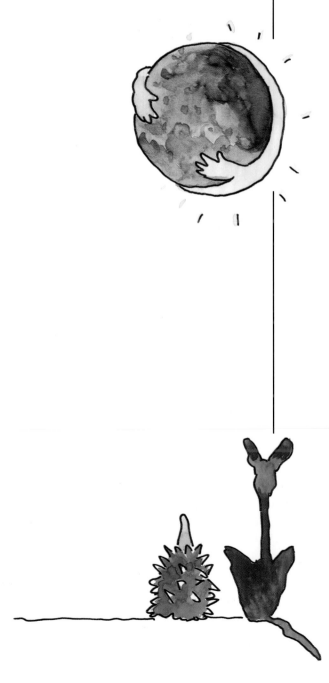

E *clipses*

Eclipse of the moon

Most years there is a chance to see an eclipse of the moon. Newspapers tell you when to expect one. They happen only at full moon: gradually a dark patch moves over the moon, then it moves away. This takes a couple of hours. If the moon is fully covered we say the eclipse is total. If not, it is a partial eclipse.

The dark part is the shadow of the earth. An eclipse of the moon can happen only if the moon moves exactly into line with the sun and the earth.

The earth's shadow may be black but usually it is orange or red. The color is caused by red light getting through the earth's atmosphere. These are sunset colors seen on the moon. The eclipse is darkest if volcanoes on earth have thrown a lot of dust into the air.

About 2500 years ago, Greek scholars worked out what happens during an eclipse of the moon. They saw that the earth's shadow was round and so realized that the earth is also round.

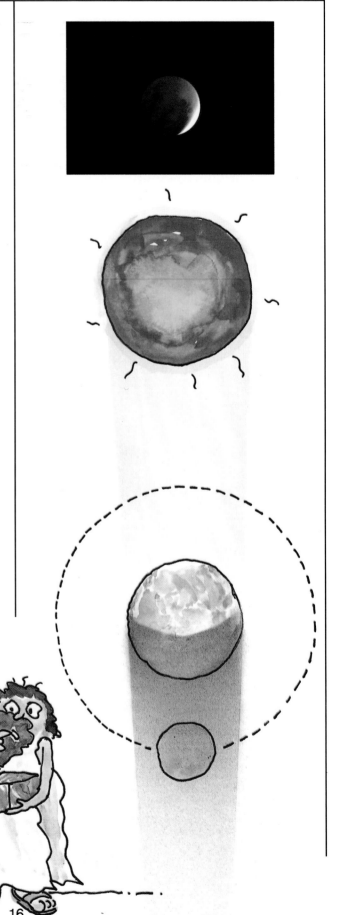

Eclipse of the sun

An eclipse of the sun is also visible most years. It happens when the moon moves between the earth and the sun, so it occurs only at new moon. If only part of the sun is covered, the eclipse is partial.

During a total eclipse, when the sun is completely hidden, we see the beautiful **corona**, a sort of atmosphere to the sun.

We also see the rosy pink prominences, like flames sticking out of the sun. These prominences are much bigger than the earth!

In olden days, people were very frightened by eclipses of the sun because they didn't know what caused them and thought that the sun might not recover.

These days many people go to watch an eclipse of the sun. If you do, remember never to stare at the sun, even to watch a partial eclipse.

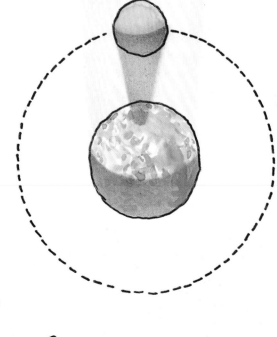

Watching the Planets

After the sun and the moon, planets are the next brightest things in the sky. From night to night they move relative to the background of stars. Five planets are easily seen. Of the five, Venus is the brightest, then Jupiter and Mars; Saturn and Mercury are the faintest.

When several planets are visible at the same time, they lie almost in line across the sky. This is because they keep close to the **ecliptic**, the path that the sun follows through the constellations of the zodiac.

Mars
Mars comes round every couple of years but is hidden by the sun for long periods in between. You can recognize Mars by its rusty orange color.

Mercury
Unless you know where to look, you might never recognize Mercury, although it often appears low in the sky just after sunset or before dawn.

Venus
You must have seen Venus. For several months it sits in the west after sunset, growing brighter day by day until it quickly zooms past the sun and appears in the morning sky. There it slowly fades, moves past the sun again and gradually appears in the evening sky to start the cycle again.

Mercury and Venus are seen only at dusk and dawn so each has been known for hundreds of years as the morning star and the evening star.

Jupiter

Jupiter is bright for several months each year. It is brightest about one month later each year, and is then visible all night.

Through a small telescope or binoculars you can see dark bands across it: these are streaks of different types of clouds. You can also see the four major moons of Jupiter. From night to night they change position, and sometimes one or two are hidden by the planet. Their names are Io, Europa, Ganymede and Callisto.

Saturn

Saturn is fainter than Jupiter but you can see the rings around it through a telescope or binoculars. Every 14 years the rings seem to disappear because they are tilted exactly edge-on to the earth. The rings are made of lumps of ice.

Some newspapers and magazines tell you where to find the planets each month.

Find a bright planet in the sky. Try drawing a map of the stars around the planet. About once a week mark on your map where the planet is. You will see how it moves.

The Planet Family

The planets are other worlds rather like the earth. What would you take with you if you went on holiday to another planet? You'd need all your food and drink, plus cylinders of compressed air because no other planet has the sort of air that we breathe.

Mars isn't too bad a spot. The red planet is covered with rusty sand and boulders, extinct volcanoes and dried-out river beds. Millions of years ago plants might have lived on Mars but now it's a lifeless desert of shifting sand.

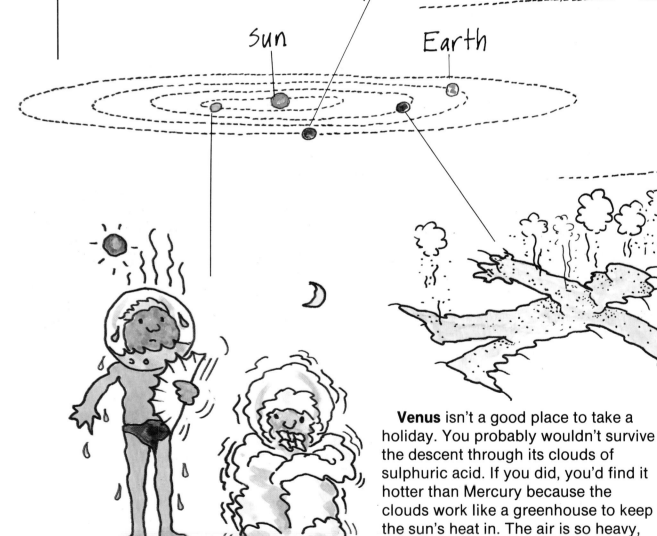

Sun

Earth

Venus isn't a good place to take a holiday. You probably wouldn't survive the descent through its clouds of sulphuric acid. If you did, you'd find it hotter than Mercury because the clouds work like a greenhouse to keep the sun's heat in. The air is so heavy, too, that you'd be crushed to death.

Mercury is so close to the sun that the temperature by day is as hot as an oven. What's more, the sun is up for three months at a time. The night also lasts three months, and it gets far colder even than the South Pole.

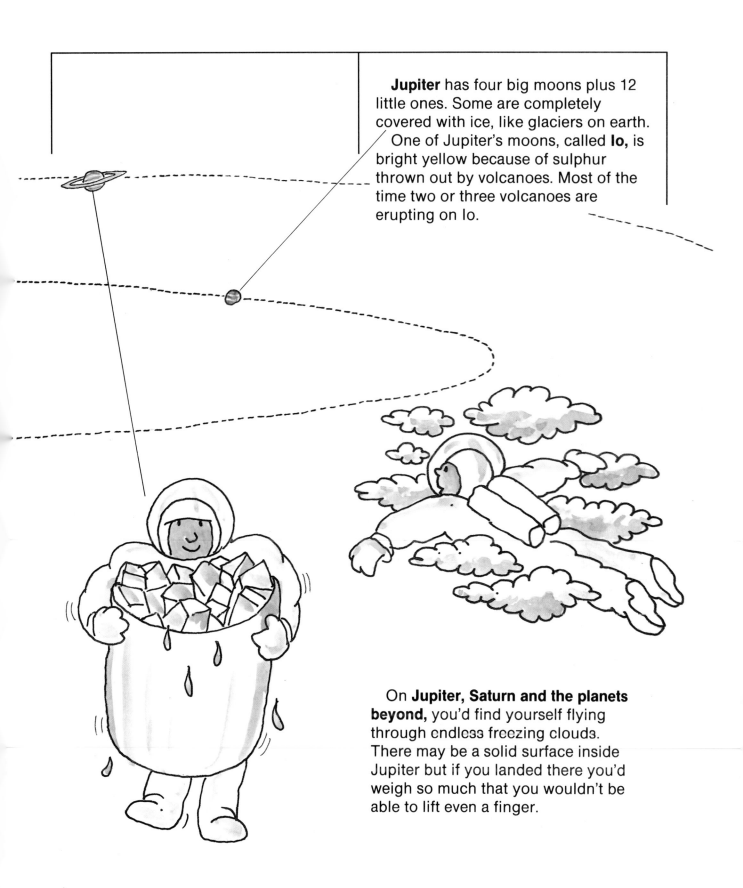

Jupiter has four big moons plus 12 little ones. Some are completely covered with ice, like glaciers on earth. One of Jupiter's moons, called **Io,** is bright yellow because of sulphur thrown out by volcanoes. Most of the time two or three volcanoes are erupting on Io.

On **Jupiter, Saturn and the planets beyond,** you'd find yourself flying through endless freezing clouds. There may be a solid surface inside Jupiter but if you landed there you'd weigh so much that you wouldn't be able to lift even a finger.

There's enough ice in the rings of **Saturn** to chill ten cold drinks a day for all the people who will ever live on earth.

Comets and Meteors

Comets

Have you ever seen a comet? Many pass by every year but only about every five years is there one bright enough to see without a telescope.

There are millions and millions of comets around the sun. We usually don't know when one will come close enough to see. Halley's comet is the only bright one that we can anticipate, and it won't come back till the year 2062.

The straight tail is made of steam and other gases that have boiled off the nucleus.

The curved tail is made of little bits of dirt that have fallen off the nucleus.

The fuzzy head is called the coma

The nucleus is a frozen blob of frost and dirt, perhaps 2 or 3 km (a mile or 2) across, but the tail can grow hundreds of millions of times longer. This is like a rat growing a 1000 km (600 mile) tail.

Meteors

Shooting stars, which astronomers call meteors, are small grains of dust burning up in the earth's atmosphere, just like many spacecraft do when they make a re-entry. The grains were left behind by comets, probably thousands of years ago.

Meteors usually burn up 100 km (60 miles) above the ground, but lumps of rock get through to ground level, sometimes making big craters where they land. When they are found we call them **meteorites**. The best place to find meteorites is on the ice of Antarctica, where there are no other rocks to confuse us.

ET in your living room!

Many meteorites burn up almost completely on their way through the atmosphere. They reach the earth's surface and are found everywhere, though they are too tiny to recognize because they look like dust. Many meteorites are made of iron, so if you were to drag a magnet around your house you might find some.

The Stars in the Sky

Constellations

The sky looks like a big dome over our heads, and it is easy to think of the stars as bright lights stuck on that dome. This is how we see them in a planetarium, and it is natural to assume that all stars are the same distance away from us.

Hundreds of years ago that is what people thought. In ancient times they also imagined that groups of stars formed pictures in the sky. They called these pictures **constellations**, and gave each one a name. They thought of the sky as a jigsaw puzzle made of constellations all fitted together on the dome.

Now we know that there is no dome in the sky. The stars are not all the same distance away, but are widely scattered at different distances. And we know that constellations are not real groups, but simply chance patterns according to how we see the stars from the earth.

We still use the constellations invented by Greek astronomers about 2000 years ago because it helps us to find our way around the sky.

The best known constellations are in the **zodiac**. These are the ones that the sun passes through every year. Each has its own special symbol.

♈ Aries, the ram

♉ Taurus, the bull

♊ Gemini, the twins

♋ Cancer, the crab

♌ Leo, the lion

♍ Virgo, the virgin

♎ Libra, the scales

♏ Scorpius, the scorpion

♐ Sagittarius, the archer

♑ Capricornus, the goat

♒ Aquarius, the water carrier

♓ Pisces, the fishes

Actually, the sun also passes through the constellation Ophiuchus, between Scorpius and Sagittarius.

Bright stars often have their own names, too. Most were named by Arab astronomers a thousand years ago. For example, the brightest star in Taurus is called Aldebaran, which means "The Follower" in Arabic.

Some Star Groups

As the earth rotates, all the stars seem to turn around a point in the sky known as the **north celestial pole**. "Celestial" means "of the sky". In the northern hemisphere there is a star known as **Polaris** or the **North Star** located at the north celestial pole. It is part of the constellation Ursa Minor.

To locate Polaris, first find a group of seven stars called the **Big Dipper**. (The Big Dipper is part of a constel-lation called Ursa Major, but it is easy to find the Big Dipper on its own.) Two stars in the Big Dipper point directly at Polaris.

Another constellation nearby is Cassiopeia, on the other side of Polaris from the Big Dipper.

All constellations have Latin words for names, though some names, like Cassiopeia, come from Greek words.

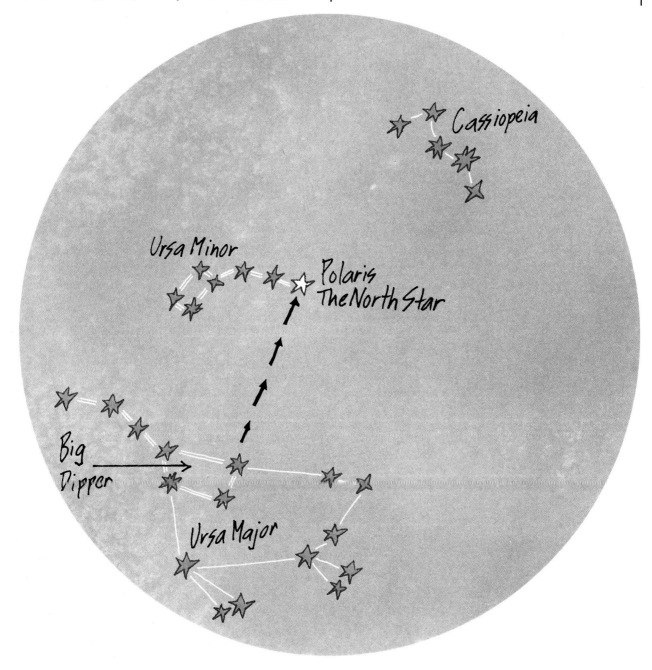

The birth of stars

Stars are made in dark, wispy clouds of gas and dust. Very slowly, over millions of years, the gas becomes concentrated in a few places and shrinks into balls. When a ball has shrunk enough, a hydrogen bomb begins to burn in its centre. The ball glows brightly: it is then a star.

The sun was made this way about 5000 million years ago. It looks different to other stars only because it is so much nearer to us.

Every star is a ball of gas, just like the sun. There are big stars and small stars, hot stars and not so hot stars. Astronomers call the big, cooler stars red giants and the small, hot stars white dwarfs. Aldebaran is a red giant.

The death of stars

Stars live for many millions of years. When they die, most just fade away.

A few very big stars die by blowing themselves to pieces as a **supernova**. The most famous supernova blew up in February 1987.

The Milky Way

The **Milky Way** is the name we give to a faint band of light that you can sometimes see stretching across the sky near the horizon. It isn't made of milk, of course, but of millions of stars that are part of our **galaxy**. The stars are very faint because they are very far away, but there are so many of them that their lights join together to make a haze of light.

A galaxy is like a giant ship filled with stars, all sailing along together in the empty ocean of space. Our sun is just one of billions of stars that make up the Milky Way galaxy. There are about as many stars in this galaxy as you could fit pins inside a house.

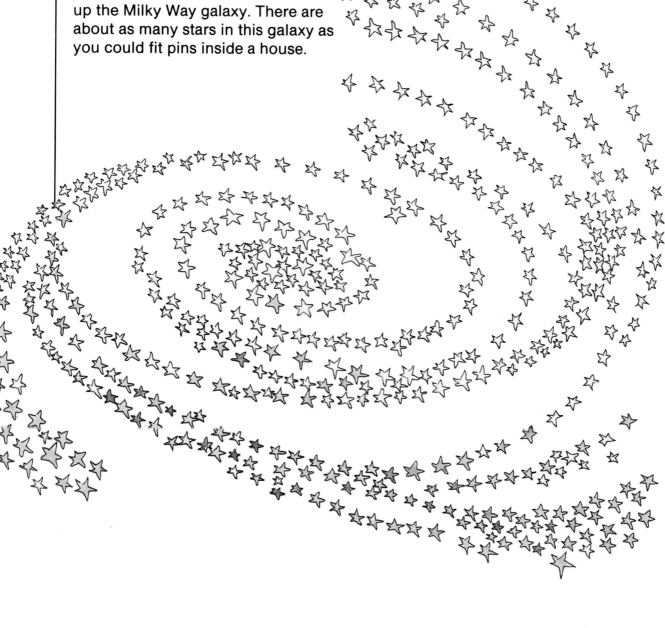

How to make your own model galaxy

Take a cup of black coffee and stir it so it is going around. Add a little cream and watch how it makes a spiral.

If you could take a flight out of our galaxy and look down on it, you'd see the stars spread out in a big spiral pattern, just like the cream in the coffee cup. Our galaxy is a spiral galaxy.

Like the coffee, our galaxy goes around, but it takes 200 million years to go around once.

On a map of our galaxy, the sun and earth would be together near the outside edge.

Seen from the edge, our galaxy is quite thin, just as the cream on the coffee is a thin layer.

Our galaxy is very, very big. Even if we could travel as fast as light it would take us 25,000 years to journey to its center. At that speed we could travel more than ten times round the earth in only one second.

Other Galaxies

The Milky Way is just one of millions of galaxies in the universe. Most are very far from us, and are rushing away at high speeds.

But that doesn't mean we have no neighbors. There are at least 20 galaxies nearby that are not moving away from us. They are our **Local Group**. Some of them may seem far away, but they are still very close compared to all the other galaxies. They are like a fleet of ships sailing together in a vast ocean.

Three of these galaxies can be seen from earth without a telescope: the **Andromeda Galaxy** and the two **Clouds of Magellan** (although the Clouds of Magellan can only be seen from the southern hemisphere). Because galaxies are made up of millions of stars, they look fuzzy or cloudy in the sky, not sharp and crisp like a star.

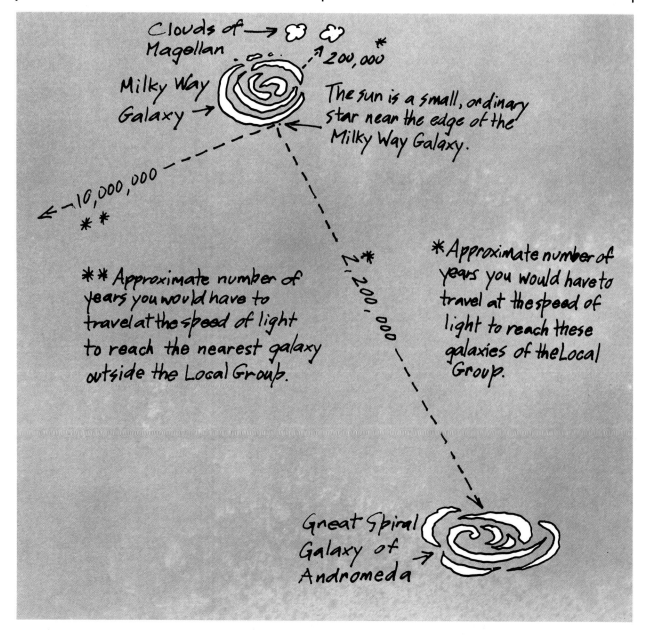

Clouds of Magellan

Milky Way Galaxy →

→ 200,000 *

The sun is a small, ordinary star near the edge of the Milky Way Galaxy.

← ~10,000,000 **

** Approximate number of years you would have to travel at the speed of light to reach the nearest galaxy outside the Local Group.

~200,000 *

* Approximate number of years you would have to travel at the speed of light to reach these galaxies of the Local Group.

Great Spiral Galaxy of Andromeda →

The Universe

There are millions of galaxies in the universe: our galaxy is just one of them. Some galaxies are bigger than ours, some are smaller. Some are spiral like our own, others are rounder, like a football. Still others are just an odd shape.

The galaxies are rushing away from one another across a universe that is over 30 thousand million light years across. Scientists think they are moving apart because of an enormous explosion that happened 15 thousand million years ago. Everything in the universe was created in that explosion. However, it took a long time for galaxies, stars and planets to form from the material of the universe. Some are still forming.

There are millions upon millions of galaxies in the universe. We live in just one of them.

There are 100 thousand million stars in that galaxy. We live near just one of them.

There are nine planets circling around that star. We live on just one of them.

There are five thousand million people on that planet. Just one of them is reading this book — you.

Seeing the Sky

Even though it would be great if you could visit an observatory to look at some of the things described in this book, you can see most of them just using your eyes. If you want to get a better look, it is best to use a pair of binoculars.

Try to use binoculars sitting in a comfortable chair that has arms on which you can rest your elbows. This stops the binoculars waving around. If you don't have a chair, find something like a wall to lean on.

Most binoculars open and close. Adjust them so that you can see the same view with both eyes.

A knob in the middle focuses the binoculars to give a crisp view. Some binoculars have separate focus for the right eyepiece. If yours have this, use the middle knob to focus your left eye, then adjust the right-eye focus with the smaller knob. If you find this difficult, it is usually good enough to set the focus on the right eye to the middle mark.

It's hard to point binoculars exactly where you want in the sky. Stare at the star you want, then move the binoculars in front of your eyes until you can see through them. Try not to move your eyes.

It is easiest to find bright stars, so work your way from bright ones to fainter ones.

Focus